Livicated to Genevieve, the perfect partner
MDS

Livicated to Michael, a very irie man
GW

First published 2003 by Little Roots
This edition published 2012 by Macmillan Children's Books
a division of Macmillan Publishers Limited
20 New Wharf Road, London N1 9RR
Basingstoke and Oxford
Associated companies throughout the world
www.panmacmillan.com

ISBN: 978-1-4472-1697-1

1 3 5 7 9 8 6 4 2

A CIP catalogue record for this book is available from the British Library.

Printed in China

Rastamouse

and the
Double-Crossin' Diva

Words by

Michael De Souza & Genevieve Webster

Pictures by

Genevieve Webster

MACMILLAN CHILDREN'S BOOKS

Check Rastamouse, Scratchy and Zoomer,
"Big up! Da Easy Crew!"
Crime-fighting, special agents,
And a super-cool reggae band too.

They're speeding past the city park,
No time to stop and play.
They're off to judge at the Talent Show
On the sands of Mousetego Bay.

The contestants come from far and wide,
The best acts throughout the land.
They compete not for fame but for fortune
ie: the prize of a hundred grand.

Downtown, the excited orphan mice
Are packing a rucksack each.
For a day at the Nuff Song Talent Show
And a night sleeping out on the beach.

Bagga Trouble, the storytime rapper,
Will be driving them all to the Show.
He picks up the keys for the minibus,
And soon they'll be ready to go.

Then outside the orphanage window,
A mouse with a bucket appears.
She speaks with a voice clear as crystal,
And this is what Bagga T hears:

"Me can clean dat ol' bus for you inside and out,
And yes, me will do dat for free.
Cos me jus' wanna do mi good deed for the day,
So jus' chill and hand me dem key."

So Bagga T thanks her, then throws her the keys
And asks if she'd mind being quick.
"Don't worry ya head 'bout dat," the mouse smiles,
"Dat's one of mi *favourite* trick!"

When the babies dance out through the orphanage door,
All set with their rucksacks on,
They look up and down the big empty street –
But the orphanage bus has gone!

Bagga T thinks it might have been stolen
By a mouse wearing blue dungarees,
As he scratches his head and remembers
The sweet voice, the smile and the keys.

So he puts in a call to the President
To tell of the terrible crime.
And tears trickle down from the orphans' eyes
As they listen to Bagga T's rhyme:

Meanwhile back at Mousetego Bay,
The curtain begins to rise
As Toots and the Mousetails take to the stage,
To compete for the hundred-grand prize.

Rastamouse says, "Dem irie man."
Scratchy and Zoomer agree,
Then a signal sounds through the radio –
A presidential emergency!

So Rastamouse jumps on his skateboard
And calls to the Easy Crew,
"Let I, Mouse, go vibes up da President
And check what him want we to do."

Then just as he reaches the exit,
Rastamouse turns back to see
A striking contestant burst onto the stage
Announcing herself . . .

... Missy D!

She spins on her head and does back-flips,
Performing a raunchy routine,
And calls out, "C'mon everybody,
Give it up for da breakdancing queen!"

Her vocals vibrate through the speakers
With a sound so dynamic and loud.
The vibe is intense and electric,
As Missy D dazzles the crowd.

Rastamouse says, "She well crucial man,
And me wish me could ah stay,
But me have to assist da President
And get dem orphan mice down to da Bay."

So he rolls straight out through the exit,
But stops suddenly when he sees
The orphanage bus that's been stolen,
Crashed into some coconut trees.

Rastamouse boards the bus and says,
"Let me check for clue 'n' ting –
But wait, hold on, what's dis me found?
Me recognize dat bling."

So our hero calls President Wensley Dale
And says, "Me have an idea,
I tink I can trap up da terrible teef,
But me need ya to come down here."

The President jumps in his limousine,
And soon he is on his way.
He picks up some V.I.P. passengers,
Then heads for Mousetego Bay.

Back at the Nuff Song Talent Show,
The contest is nearly done,
So Rastamouse secretly checks with the Crew
To see which contestant has won.

When the limo pulls up at Mousetego Bay,
Out step the V.I.P.s,
Then the President jumps up on stage and says,
"Hand me dat envelope, please."

He opens the big golden envelope,
Checking it carefully,
Then reads out loud to the expectant crowd,
"And da winner is . . .

... Missy D!"

BANK OF MOUSELAND
PAY: Missy D
One hundred grand!
$100,000

The diva takes hold of the giant cheque
To whistles and loud applause,
Then Rastamouse looks her straight in the eye,
And asks, "Is dis bling yours?"

"Yes," shrieks the winning contestant,
"Me need ya to give me dat bling.
It's one of mi lucky charms," she adds,
"And matches wid dis ears-ring!"

So Rastamouse hands it to Missy D
Saying, "Please explain to us,
Why it was on de driver's seat
Of dat stolen orphanage bus?"

"OK, it was there cos me teef dat ol' bus
Cos me love to dance 'n' sing,
And was desperate to reach ah da Talent Show,
But me nah had no money 'n' ting."

Rastamouse says, "Ya deeds was bad,
Ya really mus' tink twice,
Before ya go takin' what isn't yours
And upsettin' dem poor likkle mice."

"I'm sorry for teefin' dat ol' minibus,"
Missy D says with regret,
"Me never intended to hurt anyone,
Or leave dem poor orphan upset."

Rastamouse sees Missy D wants to change,
So he gives her some instant advice:
"Why don't ya use all dat money you won
To buy a new bus for dem mice?"

Then Rastamouse turns to the President
And whispers his crucial plan.
The President nods in agreement and –
Our hero says, "Irie, man!

Now listen up, everybody,
I 'n' da Crew gonna play,
Cos dem orphan dem missed all da music.
So nice it up, Mousetego Bay!

Get ready for reggae rock-steady,
Me hope you will join with me
In welcoming two extra-special guests . . .

. . . Missy D and Bagga T!"

Those baby mice go wild and shout,
"Da Easy Crew is da best!"
But now that the sun has nearly set,
It's time for them all to rest.

As Bagga T settles the orphans down,
Missy says, "Dat bredda sweet!"
He raps with a cool steady rhythm,
While Missy D's heart skips a beat.

As the moonlight falls on Mousetego Bay,
By the edge of the sparkling sea,
Two mice can be seen walking hand in hand –
Missy D and Bagga T.

The next day back at the orphanage,
Our hero gives Missy a chance:
"If you stop bein' a double-crossin' diva,
You can teach dem likkle orphan to dance."

Missy D is overjoyed and says,
"Me would love to do dat job.
And me promise me nah double-cross any more,
Nah teef, nah lie, nah rob."

So Missy D buys a super-cool bus
And hands Bagga Trouble the keys,
Then smiling, goes off to give her first class:
'Breakdance for Beginners' ie: babies.

"Easy Crew! Come in! Come in!
Are you reading me?
Message from President Wensley Dale,
Listen up, you three.

Ya catch dat diva cleverly,
Rastamouse, me loved ya plan.
And ya Talent Show gig was boombastic,
Or as you would say, 'IRIE MAN'."

IRIE
pronounced: i-ree
anything positive or good

BLING
pronounced: bling
expensive, shiny jewellery

DIVA
pronounced: deeva
a female singer/dancer
who likes to get her own way!

GRAND
pronounced: grand
a thousand (money)

EARS-RING
pronounced: ears-ring
an earring

V.I.P.
pronounced: vee i pee
a very important person

BOOMBASTIC
pronounced: boohm'bastik
fantastic music